THE LEGEND OF
THE
CHRISTMAS ROSE

BY WILLIAM H. HOOKS

PAINTINGS BY RICHARD A. WILLIAMS

SCHOLASTIC INC.

New York Toronto London Auckland Sydney
Mexico City New Delhi Hong Kong

ISBN 0-439-24205-3

Text copyright © 1999 by William H. Hooks. Illustrations copyright © 1999 by
Richard A. Williams. All rights reserved. Published by Scholastic Inc., 555 Broadway,
New York, NY 10012, by arrangement with HarperCollins Publishers.
SCHOLASTIC and associated logos are trademarks and/or registered
trademarks of Scholastic Inc.

12 11 10 9 8 7 6 5   2 3 4 5/0

Printed in the U.S.A.   24

First Scholastic printing, November 2000

For

Maryellen Bowers,

who introduced me to *Helleborus niger*

—W.H.

In loving memory of

Ange Weisman

—R.W.

DOROTHY had three brothers, tall and strong,
shepherd giants who guarded their father's sheep.
At least they seemed like giants to her.
Dorothy was born late,
long after the youngest of her brothers
had gone to the fields to tend the flocks.
Her mother, who had given up hope
of ever having a daughter,
named her Dorothy, which means
"gift from God."

Now in her ninth year,
Dorothy was allowed to carry a goatskin
filled with fresh water to her brothers.
But they still treated her like a small child.
"Little Dot! Little Dot!" Joab would shout.
Then he would scoop her up, toss her high
into the air, and catch her in his arms.
Micah would twirl her around and around
until she was dizzy.
"I'm not a little Dot," she would gasp.
"I'm your biggest sister."
"And you're the youngest and oldest sister, too,"
teased Jonathan.

One day when Dorothy was bringing water
to the fields, she spied strangers on the road.
Quickly, she hid until they were out of sight.
Then she rushed to her brothers.
"Did you see the strangers?" she asked.
"Do you think they are robbers?"
Micah laughed and said, "No, they are not robbers."

"All week now we have seen
many people along the road," said Joab.
"The great Roman Emperor, Augustus,
has ordered that all must return
to the city of their birth to be taxed.
Father says we should stay in the fields
and watch over the sheep tonight,
with so many strangers abroad."
"Oh," said Dorothy,
"how I'd like to sleep under the stars!"
"Well, you can't, our biggest, littlest, oldest,
and youngest sister," said Jonathan.
"Off with you, Little Dot," said Micah.
"We'll see you tomorrow morning.
And we'll be hungry as bears."

Dorothy's mother called her early,
while the morning star still was shining.
"Wake up, sleepy one, and help your mother
with the breakfast bread."
They pounded the dough into flat, round cakes.
Dorothy took the first batch outside
to bake in the clay oven.

Suddenly, through the first pale glimmering of dawn,
Dorothy saw a man running and waving his arms.
Soon he was near enough for her to hear him plainly
and to see him clearly.
"Micah!" she called. "What is wrong?"
"We have seen a host of angels!" shouted Micah.
Fast on Micah's heels came Joab, crying out,
"Glory to God in the highest!"
And then Jonathan ran up, shouting,
"We heard singing in the skies!"

Dorothy's father rushed outside.

"My sons, what has come to pass?" he asked.

All three spoke at once.

Their father raised his hand.

"Keep silent," he ordered.

"Let my eldest son, Micah, speak."

"Father, last night,

while we were watching over our flocks,

an angel of the Lord appeared.

A strange light shone around us—"

"And Father," Jonathan broke in,

"we were sore afraid!"

"Silence!" his father ordered.

"Speak on, Micah."

"It's true we were frightened, Father,
but the angel told us not to be afraid.
'Fear not,' said the angel,
'I bring you good tidings of great joy,
which shall be to all people,
for unto you is born this day
in the city of David, a Savior,
which is Christ the Lord!'"

As Micah paused for breath,
Jonathan spoke up. "Father, the angel told us
we would find the babe in a manger
in the city of David."
"That would be Bethlehem," said their father.
"The prophets have foretold this."
"Father," said Micah, "allow us to go to Bethlehem."
"Yes, my sons, the Lord has made this
known to you, and you must go.
And you must take a prize lamb
to this newborn king."

It was more than a day's journey to Bethlehem.

They would arrive after nightfall.

Dorothy and her mother scurried about

packing food for the journey,

finding the three best cloaks

and the sturdiest sandals.

How Dorothy longed to go with her brothers.

But she dared not ask,

well knowing what the answer would be.

Sadly, she watched until they were out of sight.

The moment her brothers vanished,
Dorothy's feet began to move.
It seemed she had no control over them
as they sent her running after her brothers.
All day she followed from afar,
careful not to let them see her.
She never tired or minded the hot sun,
nor did she feel any hunger or thirst.
She must see this child
of whom the prophets had foretold.
As night drew on, Dorothy feared
she might lose sight of her brothers.
And soon a greater fear struck her heart—
she had no gift for the child.
"What can I bring the babe?" she cried.
"I have not even a coin to buy a pomegranate.
What can I bring to show my love?"
Ashamed to enter the city without a gift,
Dorothy hid behind a rock and wept.

Suddenly, she heard a rush of wings
beating in the night sky.
She gazed upward
and saw, in a burst of light,
an angel waving a flower of purest white.

Dorothy covered her face and waited
until the rush of wings faded away.
When she opened her eyes,
she beheld a wondrous sight.
All of the ground surrounding the rock
was carpeted with white flowers.

She filled her arms with the snowy blossoms,
and rushed to find her brothers.
They had vanished into the dark city.
But somehow her feet guided her
through the streets to the manger.
There lay the newborn babe,
surrounded by gifts of gold, gems,
frankincense, myrrh, and a prize lamb.
Richly adorned kings stood
with three sturdy shepherds, her brothers.